BOOK 1 OF 3
KICK START YOUR PASSION AND TACKLE YOUR DREAMS

AF080803

RUSHANE J. ALLEN

BLUEROSE PUBLISHERS
India | U.K.

Copyright © Rushane J. Allen 2025

All rights reserved by author. No part of this publication may be reproduced, stored in a retrieval system or transmitted in any form or by any means, electronic, mechanical, photocopying, recording or otherwise, without the prior permission of the author. Although every precaution has been taken to verify the accuracy of the information contained herein, the publisher assumes no responsibility for any errors or omissions. No liability is assumed for damages that may result from the use of information contained within.

BlueRose Publishers takes no responsibility for any damages, losses, or liabilities that may arise from the use or misuse of the information, products, or services provided in this publication.

For permissions requests or inquiries regarding this publication, please contact:

BLUEROSE PUBLISHERS
www.BlueRoseONE.com
info@bluerosepublishers.com
+91 8882 898 898
+4407342408967

ISBN: 978-93-6783-401-5

Cover Design: Shubham
Typesetting: Sagar

First Edition: January 2025

Contents

Chapter 1
Test of Faith All on The Line 1

Chapter 2
Game Day 10

Chapter 3
The Reunion 20

Chapter 4
The Confrontation 28

Chapter 5
Facing the Fire 37

Chapter 6
Choices 43

Chapter 7
The Last Lap 51

Chapter 1
TEST OF FAITH
ALL ON THE LINE

Ashton was like any other teenage boy with dreams and aspirations of living the American dream. He fantasizes about being wealthy and taking care of his family and friends. Ashton lived in Mott Haven, New York where he and his family resided. Ashton lived with his mother Joyce, his younger brother and sister, Devaughn and Sofia, and his older brother Steven.

They lived at apartment 14 in Alloys Condo on ,47th Streak Street. Ashton went to Alame Academy, where he played football for his school. It was his last year to make a big impact in the game and earn a scholarship in order to pursue college. Growing up in Ashton's community, he had it really hard because of the bad stigma his community had.

He works at Ally's Steak House on weekends because he wanted to find a way to take care of his family, Steven usually does this but he went off to serve in the military leaving Ashton as the man of the household.

Ashton always admired his older brother because despite their surroundings and the overall environment, his older brother always had something positive to say, in other words, he was Ashton's local hero. Apart from Steven, Ashton had two friends Conny and Dre.

They were his team mates and also childhood friends. The weekend began and

Ash used it to complete his assignments and some extra work at the steak house. The night before school Ash went for a walk to the local park where he usually went with Steven to clear their minds and refocus their energy on the things that really matter in life and they would walk

and at times have a little race and the loser would do 30 push ups before he could enter the house.

But before they had their race, they would see cars and have dreams of owning them one day, Steven would even say, "The sky is the starting point where ever your imagination takes you after is where you should be and you can achieve it."

The weekend was over and the start of a new week as now commences, Ashton got up took a shower and went to school with a bright smile on his face. He also had a game Wednesday against group leaders North East Academy, they needed a win to send them on top of the group and to move onto the next round hoping to get to the state championship playoffs.

Ashton played the role of an Attacking Midfielder (AM) on his team, his friend Dre as the captain of the team played as a

Centre Back (CB) and Conny as a Striker (ST). The guys went to practice after school on Monday going over some plays with the team and coming up with new tactics. He was always the first to arrive at the training ground and the last person to leave.

He focused on perfecting his game as an attacking midfielder, and idolizes the wizard Mesut Özil and the little magician

Leo Messi with the work rate of N'golo Kante. He combined their style of play in his game making him one of the best young prospects in the league.

His coach, Mr. Murrey admired his dedication and hard work both on and off the pitch and usually compares his attitude with that of a professional player. Being the only African American on the team was challenging, so he knew he had to do the extra work because not only he wanted to be the standout player on the team but he wanted to be accepted.

Little did he know that this season would be his best season at the school because he was not only the best player on his team but to others as well, in the league. This was proven because he had the best stats on the team and undoubtedly in the league with 16 goals, 10 assists, 10/11 successful dribbles per 75 mins, 91% of successful tackles won, and 212 passes in the final third in 17 games.

He was one of the stars of the league seeking assurance of a college scholarship. Numerous colleges and scouts were keeping a close eye on him and after every game he would be approached by scouts from the most prestigious football colleges such as Clemson University, Washington, Oregon St. Wake Forest University etc.

But attending any one of those colleges all depends on his team reaching the state championship playoffs. So, his mother always encouraged him to focus on the academic side as much as he focused on molding his game to perfection. Ashton had a lot of fans and was undoubtedly one of the best players to ever attend Alame Academy, so he was admired by a lot of girls from his school but his heart was already captured by Alecia Renolds.

A student who is also the headmaster's daughter. Alecia was already off the market with Conny, Ashton's best friend. Both Conny and Dre always teased Ashton about him being shy that's why he doesn't have a girlfriend but Ash wasn't even flustered because he knew he could approach any female he wanted but, in his opinion, only one was valuable enough but he valued his friendship more so he turned his eyes and focused more on his training and studies.

It was Tuesday the day before the big game and Ash was on the field doing some drills despite getting the day off from training for Wednesday. Trenton was throwing a party after school and Coach Murrey spoke about it and forbade his squad from going because they would need their strength for the game tomorrow and they agreed.

Later that day, the guys went on their way home individually. Ash got home and talked to his mom for a while, had dinner and went back to his room where he got a shower and watched some clips of his opponent's game play and key players for tomorrow's game. At about 10:15pm, that night Ash got a notification on Instagram where he saw an Instagram live with Conny, Dre and a couple of his teammates having a blast at the party.

Ashton felt so betrayed by his best friends that he logged off, plugged in his ear pods and started to do some core work before he took a shower and went to bed. Ash woke up in the morning and was feeling rejuvenated and hydrated. He got out of bed, went to the bathroom, looked in the mirror and said, "Today Will Be A Great And Successful Day. I Claim It In The Name Of The Lord And Saviour." His mother heard him smile and she said, "Boy I know you ain't forgot to say Amen." He then smiled and whispered, "Amen."

Ash then got dressed, had breakfast and went off to school. He got to school and saw Conny and Dre in the hall and went over to them saying I'm really disappointed in you guys and walked to class. He had only two classes that day where he met up with Alecia, who sat beside him talking about Conny's behavior lately and how she felt about Conny and Ash. Despite being angry at Conny, she encouraged her to speak to him about how she felt hoping he would understand more about her state of mind and hopefully he would provide the comfort she needed.

She hugged Ash and told him, "You're a great person. Thanks so much for the advice and all the best for tonight," and kept on taking notes. After class, Ash went to the meeting area where he waited for his teammates with his coach speaking about the game and some of the key players on their squad while speaking about some tactics.

The team then approached, Mr. Murrey stood up and the squad started talking about the game but coach Murrey kept silent as a lamb in the dressing room.

He then broke his silence by saying, "May I have your undivided attention? As you gentlemen know we have a must win game today in order to make it to the playoffs to the state championship." The squad shouted, "Wooooo!! Yes sir!!" He then spun the match board where he always wrote down the starting 11 before the game. The guys got excited and were shocked after seeing the starting line-up.

Starting Line-Up

1. GK- Deandre Steele
3. CB- Joe Douglas
5. CB- George Ruddy
13. LB- Rolando Small
2. RB- Adrian Peterson
8. CM- Michael Brooks
6. CM- Maleek Walls
10. CAM- Ashton Allen (C) (Ash)
22. RM- Xavier Henry
11. LM- John Headley
18. CF- Martin Michelson

Substitution

27. GK- Liam Brown

40. GK- Jacob Henderson

4. CB- Andre Johnson (Dre)

33. CB- Elijah Reed

20. CM- William Hill

14. DM- Noah Green

25. CAM- Oliver Drake

9. ST- Conroy Wilson (Conny)

7. RM- Lucas Naldo

15. LM- Benjamin Grover

23. CAM- James Love

66. RB- Daniel Logan

16. LB- Christian Trump

27. CM- Treyon James (Trenton)

They were shocked because four (5) of the regular starters were on the bench including the captain and star center half Andre (Dre) Jackson, prolific goal scorer Conroy (Conny) Wilson with 17 goals in 15 games, Lucas Naldo, Treyon James (Trenton) and Noah Green.

The dressing room went silent for a minute and Coach Murrey said, "You guys might be thinking that the coach is crazy because I benched our Captain and 4 other key players but I believe in respect and credibility. Show hands of those who did not go to the party last night after we agreed not to. Ok, this is where respect and credibility comes into play because if I haven't drawn a line on the things that can and cannot be overlooked I wouldn't be respected and other team members would have it in their minds that they can deceive their team members or I had favorites on the team and that's far from the truth." Christian raised his hand. Coach Murrey, "Speak Trump." He said, " But coach, you made it clear that this is a must win game and some of us need this win because it's our last year and scouts will be out, we need this to go pro."

There were a couple of mumbling around the dressing room. Coach Murrey Smiled and said, "Let me teach you something in life son. "Knowledge Will Give You Power, But Character Respect." ~ By Bruce Lee. You might ask why Mr. Murrey is talking to us about Bruce Lee and we are talking about football but after the game you will understand what is meant.

The guys then gathered together and said the Lord's prayer geared up and went to the pitch. Conny and Dre were so upset about the decision their coach made to sit them on the benched. Ash went to coach and said, "Coach, why are you benching Conny and Dre? He's the captain coached." Murrey replied, " Ash look at the match board whose name is assigned to the captain's arm-band?" He replied, "But coach", "but coach nothing I believe in you and it's quite obvious that your teammates share the same belief, you need to believe in yourself. Also, great leaders are made through tough circumstances don't you ever forget that now go out there and show them why we are called the Lions."

Ash lost all fear at that point and went out on the pitch where he saw Conny, Dre, Naldo, Trenton and Noah having their own little private circle on the pitch and Ash said, "Hey guys I know you are upset but it's not a good look that our team looks segregated before the game please guys let's warm up as a team." Dre laughed and said, "Look at this guy one game in my armband and already giving us a speech on teamwork and what's right from, what's wrong get over yourself. I am the only reason you're even a part of this team I brought you guys this far let's see how you do without us", and started laughing.

"I thought you were my friend Dre you should be motivating us as the team Captain even if you are not in the captain's armband. I never saw you as less without the armband. You want it so much here you can have it. I don't need the armband to believe in myself and lead my team. Conny I am disappointed in you guys," and ran off a couple minutes after Dre and all the guys joined the team and started the pre-game warm up and were having a laugh and enjoying the warm up.

They were then signaled to the dressing room where the game would commence in 20 minutes. The guys geared up and Ash motivated the team and they applauded the talk and went into the tunnel where they met the other team with national U19 captain Gregg White and 3 other national players in the starting line-up including, last year's leading goal scorer and this year's runner up behind Conny, Stefan Wright.

Chapter 2
GAME DAY

Both teams lined up accordingly and the spectators were asked to stand for the national anthem which rang out in the stadium full of mixed emotions for the game of the seasons as some would have it.

Then they shook hands and the captains were asked to stay. Gregg won the coin toss and chose to keep the ball. The game was about to begin moments before the whistle was blown everyone took a knee promoting that there is #NOROOMFORRACISM#. The whistle then blew where Stewart knocked the ball to Antwayne Morrison U19 national midfielder who then knocked the ball to his Captain, who then knocked it to his left wing back who played it back in the midfield to Carson Brown.

The North East Academy boys were keeping possession for about 3 minutes before they started to attack their opponents. Carson Brown to Alexander Grove; he then moves past Walls, gets past Brooks and passes it to Kendrick Blue who tees up a shot that was blocked last minute and turned behind for a corner by Joe Douglas.

North East Academy has a great chance of going ahead with the aerial threat they have in Gregg White and Howard Larmond; without their captain who has won 98% of aerial duels throughout the league, they are at a disadvantage.

Trent Neil went over to take the corner for North East Academy and he stepped up and got it across at the edge of the six-yard box. Ash began shouting, "Away! Away! Away!" Luckily the ball fell to his feet where he began counterattacking. It was a 3v3 battle on the counter attack and Ash kept on dribbling Joseph Randall, who committed and Ash got past him Johnny Bruce made an attempt. Ash got pass him also and made the pass to Xavier Henry who then lobbed the ball into the eighteen-yard box to Rolando. Small out came national U19 goalkeeper Jonas (JJ) Jones to narrow the angle on small who laid it back on top for Ashton Allen who fires it into an empty net from 13 yards out.

"Goooooaaaaaaallllllllll!!!!!!" It's 1-0 to Alame Academy through replacement captain Ashton Allen. The stadium erupted as the coaching staff and his teammates on the bench went to celebrate with Ash and the others at the corner flag. Commentators, "1-0 to Alame Academy with just 27 minutes in the game, if you're just joining us on our live stream, it's one nothing to Alame Academy over North East Academy through Ashton Allen in the twenty seventh minute."

North East Academy began to press immensely through the first half but it was up until the 43 minute they got their break through Stefan Wright who scored poachers goal 5 yards out from a wicked ball across in the 6 yards box from Trent Neil.

Earlier that day, Ash's cousin Treyon had come to town while he was at school to spend a couple of months with him and his family because his father passed away Ashton's uncle Troy, his mother's older brother and Treyon was alone at the house. Treyon and Ash were really close in their childhood days until Ash's uncle Troy moved all the way to California, Sacramento for a Job as a real estate agent.

Ash and Treyon were devastated by the move and grew apart over the past few years, they haven't seen each other. Treyon was eager to meet Ash and his aunt Joyce. Joyce told Treyon thatAsh had a game tonight and if he wanted to watch the game. and he said, "Yes, I would love to," as Treyon also played football for his college team in California. He was 2 years older than Ash and played for Clamord University as a Striker.

He was the leading goal scorer for his college team in his first season and the second season will begin in a couple of months right after Ashton's graduation. So he was eager to get to the game and watch his younger cousin play. He also had a thought to record the match and send his coach at Clamord because he always told him about his younger cousin who played for Alame Academy trying to convince him to watch a game but his coach was too busy to ever give it a thought, so he wanted to convince his coach even more about giving Ash a full scholarship to Clamord University.

The game was locked 1, a piece between the two teams going into the second half the score was flattering because no one could've thought it would be such a tightly match game because

North East Academy won state championship last year and the year before, so they were the overall favorites to advance. "ASH!!! ASH!!!," a familiar voice shouting out of the blue he looked up and saw his cousin Treyon shouting his name from the bleachers stand. He waved with a wide grin feeling rejuvenated seeing his cousin/best friend and his mom with his younger siblings. Ash then walked to the tunnel to the dressing room where his coach went to speak about the first half of the game and what they can work on improving for a victorious second (2nd) half.

Coach Murrey drew up the game plan in the second half and he still didn't include his 4 stars on the bench. He had faith in the team he put out there to get the job done and everyone except Dre agreed to the game play and everyone accepting Ash as the new team captain. He was far from happy with his best friend being team captain.

He handed out the water bottles to his teammates with a very distain look on his face. He then handed his best friend Ash his water who replied, "Thank You Dre." He walked away without saying anything to Ash. The guys then made their way onto the pitch where Ash was met his cousin Treyon in the tunnel, who exchanged hug with his long lost best friend and gave him some advice and motivation for the second half.

Ash smiled and was going in on the second half on a high. "The two teams are out and the second 45 will Commence now," said the commentators. "Phew!!!," Martin Michelson to Ash who attempt to go forward then played the ball to his Wing Back who played it to his Centre Half knocking the ball around before a long ball was played over to his Left Midfielder John Headley on the overlap who burst pass his opponent down to the corner flag who hooked back a brilliant ball on top arriving Ashton who had a beautiful left foot.

He came in setting up to take the shot. The goal keeper anticipating the shot defenders getting ready to put their body on the line. Ash then disguised a wonder ball to his left back on the overlap splitting the back line in half, even the commentators didn't see that wonder pass.

The goalkeeper was left on his backside along with couple of his defenders who didn't expect Ashton to make such a world class play. His left back Rolando Small had an open net begging to be hit with the ball that was played he couldn't have had an easier goal in his entire career the transition of this play was so smooth everyone was in awe, when Rolando strikes the ball in the back of the net with authority the stadium erupted even the opposition coach and fans were in awe with what they saw.

They had to applaud the stroke of genius they saw from the 18 years old playmaker. His cousin stood up shouting "Özil", referring to his younger cousin comparing the play with one of the famous playmaker's Mesut Özil. The crowd joined in shouting on the top of their voices, "Özil!!! Özil!!!! Özil!!!" Ash celebrated with his teammates and then urged them to get back to position and keep their focus because the game is far from over.

The guys regroup and get back into their respective positions, waiting for the game to restart. The guys were hit with a wave of attacks from North East Academy till 73 mins where something devastating happened. Treyon had run to the bathroom which was located in the Tunnel where he passed Dre leaving out of the dressing room both guys nod their head acknowledging each other.

Treyon was wondering, why was a team member in the tunnel while the match was in effect but he never really gave it a serious thought he then went back to the stands and continued supporting his younger cousin. The game continued with the same intensity and aggression from both teams but majority of the ball possession was with North Academy setting the pace of the game pushing

Alame Academy on the back foot. Ash was doing overtime on both offensive and defensive third.

He began to encourage his teammates to stay focus and keep track of their markers. North East Academy attempted a through pass where Xavier Henry played it to Ash on top of the 18yard box who dribbled pass 1 beats two he is still going, Ashton Allen is going what an incredible dribble, passes it out wide to Adrian Peterson on the overlap who then takes on the opponents left back and wins due to sheer pace and power.

Ash leading the charge had to readjust because the ball was played slightly behind him. Gregg White managed to get a flick on only pushing the ball further behind Ash who has already readjusted with a bicycle kick 2 yards behind the penalty spot hitting the ball so perfectly into the top corner, leaving the goalkeeper flat foot and the crowd in awe.

Even the opposition fans stand and applauded the brilliance of this young playmaker, "He dreamt of it!! he made and turn his boyhood dream into a reality the audacity to portray and finish off a move so smooth is staggering a goal of a lifetime. Ashton Allen a boy who is a star!!!" It was the 83rd minute so the game was far from over Gregg White scored cutting the two goal deposits and kept on motivating his team that there is still time for them to turn this.

Ash gathered the boys and told them "Hey, we are currently leading by a goal. We need to focus on winning back possession and keeping the ball." The whistle blew the game restarted and the team began to press the ball. The plan was to press the ball for the first 15 seconds. If it wasn't recovered by then, they would stop and get back in shape, which they did after an unsuccessful 15 seconds of high pressing.

North East Academy went on the front foot after 32 successful passes were made in the oppositions half then a quick ball was played over the top to their talisman Stefan Wright who put the ball in the back of the net with 2 minutes plus injury time to spare. It was game on at that point.

Conroy got flustered because Stefan Wright had just drawn level with him on the goal scoring chart but he got no one but himself to blame on that part. Treyon continued wondering why was that player in the tunnel when the game had commenced but he was more focused on the game at hand while making short clips to send his coach to recruit his cousin.

The game continued while North East Academy kept on knocking on the door with the game locked at 3 a piece up until the 90th minute where they were given 4 minutes stoppage time which seemed like an eternity to the Alame Academy boys who kept their opponents shut out until they got a corner kick in the dying embers of the game which resulted in a penalty kick and Joe Douglas getting send off for illegally stopping a clear goal scoring header from Gregg White with his hands from 2 yards out from the goal line giving the North East Academy boys a lifeline through their Talisman Stefan Wright who was on a hattrick.

The game was interrupted and both teams and their respective benches started to go at it which led to several yellow cards been issued out before the captains gathered their teammates full of mixed emotions about what Joe Douglas did.

Some saw it has a heroic decision while on the other hand an unsportsmanlike act but either way his actions will be justified by this one kick of the ball. "And Stefan Wright with the most important kick of the game probably his career at this point," Commentators **"Phwwwwwhht" the referee's whistle echoed across the stadium and he steps up and he hits the post and Rolando Small clears the ball!!!** making a successful pass to Ashton who was furthest up the field locked in a 2v1 position facing Gregg White and Joshua Smith.

He dribbles 2 steps over and leaves Joshua Smith on his backside. Now he is facing Gregg White who keeps on backing off waiting on the perfect moment to commit a tackle Ashton goes on until he's 22 yards from goal facing the best defender in the league.

Everyone held their breath wondering how this attack would play out. Gregg White already on a yellow card doesn't want to take him down resulting in an automatic suspension so he is currently thinking and trying to find an opening. The crowd grew silent. Ashton who was a master of fake shots had it in his mind and he turned his body setting up like he is going to the far post. Gregg White thought he saw an opening and committed which was exactly what Ashton was hoping for while thinking about the fake shot.

Gregg White committed. He scopes the ball over his feet. Gregg White who saw that he had no chance winning the ball, grabs his Jersey ripping it off him, while his goalkeeper Jonas came pouncing making himself big, seeing his Captain sacrificing himself trying not to make Ashton score who immediately saw the keeper coming full force for both him and ball. He then fake the shot while still being held back by Gregg White before being hauled to the ground.

He slots it with the outside of his left boot inside the far-right corner the stadium erupted causing mayhem. Inside the stands commentators jumping up and down in their booth. Coach Murrey couldn't believe his eyes; while everyone on the bench went wild running onto the pitch seeing such extraordinary display leading to the goal and securing all 3 points and a state championship playoff spot.

They hugged him, some kiss him on his cheek but Ashton Allen is the untold hero tonight. The game restarted after all the wild celebrations for one last time. Everyone from Alame Academy bench stood on the line waiting for the kick off so that the whistle can be blown for one last time.

"Whistle" they took a shot from the half way line desperately looking for a lifeline but the ball flew over the net. The referee then held both his hands up whistle in his mouth, "Phwwwhht, Phwwwhht, Phwwwwwwwhht!!!" Signaling the game came to an end.

The Alame Academy boys ran onto the pitch towards their hero and captain of the day while some of the North East

Academy boys fell to their knees in defeat and some laying on their backs thinking about where they fell short. The headmaster of Alame Academy was in a very jovial mood and went to the locker room and gave the guys a speech before heading to his office where he saw a note saying "Turn On Your Laptop."

He was shocked and somewhat scared so he looked around in his office before turning on his laptop. He turned it on and saw a video of his daughter doing drugs on camera at Trenton's party. He fell back in his chair flabbergasted, then his office phone rang and someone said, "If you want your daughter to live a normal life and have a chance to attend Yale, meet me 6pm @ Jack's which is a restaurant everyone goes to for business meetings etc."

The voice then said, "Don't be late." Before he could ask who is this, the person said "And come alone" and hang up. The headmaster sat back down and thought how will he sweep this under the carpet.

Chapter 3
THE REUNION

Ashton finally got out of the locker room and went outside where he saw his cousin waiting for him at the exit of the school campus, He asked; "where is mom, Devaughn and Sofia?"

"They left because Sofia and Devaughn have school in the morning so I told them I would wait for you here on the campus. But that's not the way to greet your older cousin." And they hugged and started to head home. The next morning Ashton woke up very eager to go to school. He even got up before the alarm, took a shower, pray and got dress so he was earlier than the regular time he normally went to school. While entering the campus each football player was given a cheer upon their arrival. Some of the players even joined and cheer for their teammates.

This gives the team a boost in morals. Majority of the players were on the campus which leaves Ashton and his best friends who haven't reconciled the issue that went down before the game. Yesterday Ashton went to visit his 2 best friends as usual before going to school and saw both Dre and Conny outside sitting down not dressed for school so he went to them and said; "So you guys are too big for school now I see." Dre replied; "Look who it is, Captain fantastic the man of the moment," Conny kept silent so Ashton said; "Don't tell me you're still in your feelings over what took place yesterday," he remained unbothered then Ashton said to Dre, "Gregg White was a beast in last night's game", Dre replied; "I would have scored at least 2 last night if I was playing."

They kept on talking until Conny broke silence and said; "Don't flatter yourself you played well but we conceded too many goals." To which Ash replied; "If only we had a center half, good enough to read the game and break up these plays." Conny replied; " You think that you're funny, right?" He got a phone call from Brooklyn which is his ex- girlfriend. Ashton saw it but didn't say anything. "So, aren't you guys going to school or not?" Conny went inside and Dre went next door given that they are neighbors, got dressed and drove to school.

They arrived 10 minutes later and came to a homecoming with everyone screaming, "Ashton!!! Ashton!!! Ashton!!!" while others welcome both Dre and Conny gracefully. It was Ashton who was the star of the moment who carried his team to State championship playoffs for the first time in their history he was like a living legend at his school well respected by his peers and teachers, being brilliant both on and off the pitch. He was set on his way in becoming a superstar. Scouts from all over the country began reaching out to his coach and his mother with offers but it was all up to him told by his mother and his coach which offer suits him the best.

Ashton went to the stands at recess by himself just looking out of place vibing with his earpods in his ears listening to his favorite artist Rod Wave-(2019) before Alecia saw him and sat beside him. He removed his ear pods, then she said; "May I have a your autograph Mr. Allen." He smiled and asked he "what's up;" "Just here I just broke up with your friend" he asked; "Why? What happened;" "I don't wanna talk about it, I just wanna clear my mind and refocus on the things that really matters." "OK what's on your mind?" "I don't really know, you wanna ditch school and go for a drive," "Sure that sounds fun" " OK let's go." And they went for a drive.

They arrived at their destination on top of a hill where they can see the city at its peak beauty. They both took a sigh of relief with the wind in their hair having a small meaningless conversation with the city's beauty in their sights. "I wanna," they spoke at the same time both, started smiling while telling the other to go ahead, "Ladies before gentlemen, I was taught by my mother." She smiled and said, "I needed this. It is very refreshing even though I know to skip school isn't going to go well when our parents find out." They laughed, "-I'm sorry, things didn't work out with Conny," "That's ok it was probably for the best."

They kept on talking until there was an awkward moment of silence. They started to look at each other with lust in their eyes both craving the lips of each other. They leaned towards each other then, the rain came showering down so they got up and rush back into the car before getting soaked breaking the concentration between them in that awkward moment and they head back home.

Meanwhile at the school, the headmaster confided in his best friend Jack Palmer who is a police officer about the video he got about his daughter and what the other person requested from him, to meet them at Jack's which his friend told him it is public place with camera so he thinks he'll be safe and he'll set up a parameter surrounding the entire restaurant so the person block mailing him has nowhere to run to and they can bring him in for questioning. They agreed to the plan while patiently waiting on time.

Ashton's mom was at home with his younger siblings and Trey, talking about his grades and everything and which college would be best for him both career wise and academically but the decision was always up to him at the end of the day. Trey and his aunty talked for a few more minutes before they settled in for dinner. The front door finally opened, and to their surprise it wasn't Ashton but his hometown hero is older brother Steven who came home from deployment.

His mother broke down in tears as she saw her first born, her eldest child, her rock when she needed him. She rushed to him and gave him a big hug which led tears to fall from his eyes, seeing his siblings and mom for the first time since he got deployed. His younger siblings joined giving their older brother a hug. He then asked; "Where's Ash?" His mother replied, "He is not yet home from school but looking at the time, I think he will be home soon." Ashton was caught up in his mind on his way home thinking about the day he spent with Alecia.

He was so infatuated that he logged onto Tiktok and kept on looking at her photos and videos for quite sometimes, that he almost missed his stop. He approached his door and heard a familiar voice and opened the door. He saw his older brother looked at him and then went upstairs to his room.

His cousin said, "What's that all about?" She replied, "Just give him sometime Steven he'll come around" he shocked his head and went to his room. Everyone went to their respective areas. The following morning Ashton stayed in his room when his mother called for breakfast. Steven got up early and looked after breakfast for everyone hoping to make amend with Ashton.

Ashton stayed in his room until it was time for him to head to school. He came down, wished everyone a good morning, gave his mother a kiss on her cheek, spoke to his cousin for a bit, gave his younger brother a pat on the head, pull his baby sister's cheek and walked with Steven who had his hand held out. Trey who was so confused said to his aunt and Steven, "OK aunty can someone explain to me what is really going on here?" She sighed then brought out both Devaughn and Sofia to the school bus then told Trey, "Ok, let's get it over with."

Meanwhile Alecia got a call from her father to report to the head-masters office before class began and she went without hesitation not knowing what awaits her. She reached the headmasters office and before she could ring the door it opened where she saw her father, mother and his best friend /detective and said, "Am I in trouble because I can explain" her mother replied, "Ohh young lady you got lots of explaining to do," she swallowed deeply and looked at her parents.

Ashton arrived at school feeling very elated but somewhat sad because he was at a point in life where everything is going great in is academic and sports life but it feels like everything is crumbling down on his personal life so it was like he's at a stalemate in his life and this could affect his performance on the pitch. His coach saw this and called him and said, "what's going on Ash it's like your here physically but mentally on a different planet what's going on?" "I'm good coach just thinking about the playoffs and some family issues so it's a little crowded in my mind right now," "Walk with me" and they started walking towards the football pitch and his coach said,

"Be honest when you look at the pitch what comes to your mind and how does it makes you feel knowing that you got 90 minutes plus stoppage time to showcase your talent and let it all out on this pitch?" Ashton took a second to grasped what his coach just said then he replied, "Well coach to be honest with you, when I see the pitch I yell freedom in my mind because this is the only time I get to show the side of me nobody knows exist and whenever I get the chance to play nothing matters or is more important within that 90 minutes. It's like the world could be on fire and I wouldn't realize until those 90 minutes are up because that's how I escape reality."

His coach smiled and said, "The passion you have for this sport reminds me of myself but don't make the same mistakes I made. You can't save everyone in your life some you got to leave behind and some you have to watch try and save themselves before you offer your assistance so therefore live your life in your accordance and don't carry any extra baggage in your heart towards anyone, instead live, accept, adapt, forgive and grow and you will live a happy and peaceful life.

He looked at his coach and shook his head then the bell rang for class time and head back down the tunnel for class, leaving his coach on the pitch. Ashton went to class feeling an ease having just spoke to his coach and he was happy to see Alecia which by surprise she wasn't there in class which left him wondering. She was in the headmaster's office explaining herself about what took place at the party the other night. She began to talk before anyone could ask her any question, "Let me explain, I talked Ashton into leaving school early because I wanted to free my mind so if there's anyone to blame it's me." Her father and mother replied, " You did what?!!!" She looked surprised, "So what am I here for if it's not for leaving school before class is over?" Her mother replied "Look at this video," her father turned around the laptop showing her the video of her doing drugs at Trenton's party. Her face went pale for about 5 seconds before tears started rolling down her cheeks.

She never felt so embarrassed in her life. Seeing herself like that wasn't something she ever thought would ever happen because she was so focused on what is important in life and for her future. "LET'S HEAR THE EXPLANATION!!!" Her mother exclaimed while looking at her daughter heartbroken. She stuttered before she could form the words in proper sentences, "I..I...I never thought..." before she could finish her father said, "Of course, you never thought because you weren't aware of the consequences. You were just thinking about having a good time getting in the zone. Is that what you teenagers called it these days?" He asked sarcastically, she replied; "I didn't know that I was being recorded. I swear, I wouldn't jeopardize my future like that I was just trying to get over the fact that me and Conny broke up. Mom, Dad you got to believe me." Her mother looked at her and felt deep remorse of seeing her daughter crying like that and hugged her and said; "You know, you can always talk to me, Munchkin. Why do you think doing drugs would be the right solution. Don't worry we'll fix it, Munchkin we'll fix it." Her father got so angry. He knock down on his desk and turned to Jack and said; "How long do I have before the meeting?" Jack said, "2 hours 3 minutes" "Ok good" Hearing the conversation Alecia replied what meeting is that. Her father looked at her and said you've done enough. I'll take it from her where this is regard. I don't want you to get involved and as for skipping school you and Ashton have 1 week in school suspension no extra curriculum activities that means no chess club and no watching match on Friday and I will call Ashton's mother letting her know he skipped school and he has a 1 match suspension." Alecia begged her father not to punish Ashton because she was the one with the idea of ditching school and she forced him and he was only there because he wanted to keep her safe.

Her father told her that's final and she should head back to class. Later that day Ashton was informed about his suspension and the severity of it. Alecia heard and was looking for him the entire day because she felt responsible for what had happened. She searched the entire school and couldn't find him then she remembered him talking about a spot in the park where he and his older brother Steven would go when he was younger to get away from all the problems at end. She went down there where she saw Ashton sitting on the bench just looking out of place.

He looked so sad that she was surprised that there weren't any tears in his eyes. She approached him gently and said, "May I take a seat?" he looked up and said; "You can sit wherever you want it's not my bench." She replied "I know you are angry and believe me I would be too. I even tried to tell my father it was my idea and to punish me and not you, but he wasn't having it but if there's anything that I can do believe me, I would." He smiled and said, "I don't blame you, Alecia. I blame myself because I knew better and my reward is to sit out the match on Friday."

She told him she would try and talk some sense to her father but it would not be easy. Ashton was only listening because he likes her and it would only hurt her feelings even more, if he would agree that it was her to blame for his suspension.

Chapter 4
THE CONFRONTATION

Meanwhile Ashton's mom was at home explaining to Treyon about the bad blood between Ashton and his brother Steven. "Ok Trey, it all started when Steven got the call that he was accepted as a Marine in the U.S. army and that he should report for training in the next 2 weeks. He was so happy that he told me but he hid it from Ashton who looked up to his older brother and told him everything and for Steven to keep a secret like that from him.

He was devastated because his birthday was the day after Steven left which he had no Idea, that his brother would leave. He made so many plans for his birthday with his brother being the emphasis of everything. So, when his mother told him, Steven was gone. He felt so betrayed that he didn't know he got accepted and left without telling him goodbye but Steven didn't know how to break his baby's brother heart and went on and left without seeing him.

So, that's why he is reluctant to speak with his brother. Trey felt a little heart warmth to the situation and encouraged Steven to speak to Ashton to clarify and explain what really happened and how sorry he was for how things went down." Steven replied, " What if he doesn't want to speak to me?" Trey said "The truth is he doesn't but not speaking to him hurts even more." He shook his head took up his jacket and went looking for Ashton after Trey gave him some clues on where here he would be able to find his brother.

Trey went on to search for Ashton at his favorite spots without success and then it came to him on where he might find his brother. So he went on to the park where he last spoke to his brother and found him sitting on the bench. "So, we ignoring each other now," Steven uttered, "You should be an expert on that, right?" Look Ash, I am so sorry for not letting you know that I was leaving." "OK apology accepted. Can you please go now?" Ashton spoke sarcastically. "Look, how can I make it back up to you?" "It's a little too late for that, big bro." He got up and walked away while Steven sat down looking depressed on the bench.

Ashton woke up the morning and found his older brother Steven at his door waiting for him with his sneakers and water bottle. He wondered how did he know that I needed them. Steven was briefed about his morning routine by their mother who gave Steven some ideas on how they could reconnect and save their brotherhood with these gestures. Ash took the sneakers and water bottle and they both went down stairs and heard a voice coming from the kitchen, "What took you guys so long? I know you were not thinking of leaving me, right?" Said Trey.

All 3 boys went on outside to do some cardio then hit the gym afterwards. On the other hand, Alecia went on speaking to her father about lifting Ashton's match ban on Friday because it would be a life and career changing game for Ash and his family but her father was so in rage that he just walked out before she could finish what she had to say. Her mom said just give him some time, I'll speak to him in the meantime.

Go get ready for school, I'll drop you off shortly. She usually travels with her dad but because of the bad blood between them her mother decided to take her to school than to make it worse because they are a splitting image of each other. USADA came to Ash school that day which is the United States Anti-Doping Agency to run some tests on the players leading up to the game on Friday. Everyone gather where they were put through a series of test and data gathering by the USADA. Coach Murrey will receive the results on Wednesday where he would see the squad eligibility after the results were in which he was 100% sure that he would have a full squad depth to choose from coming this Friday.

The team went to training the following day where everyone was on their A game trying to secure a spot in the starting 11. Coach Murrey decided to make Ash the captain, despite the return of Dre. "Alright guys, our Captain for the match upcoming this Friday remains. So, Ashton you'll lead this team going into the final." "Ok coach" said Ash. Despite being the vice-captain, Dre went over to congratulate Ashton on his new role and at the same time to give him some advice. Coach Murrey knew from the start that Ash was the best person to captain the team. He didn't let him have the armband because he wanted him to get him out of his shell and step up to the plate which he is doing right now.

He has been more vocal, virtuous, little of a maverick and very passionate about his players and their work rate both on and off the pitch, which leads him to be the best person for the Job. He went home that day and share the news with his mum. Treyon and siblings, they were all supportive towards him. Alicia's mom spoke to her husband about the match ban that he gave Ash. He was somewhat relaxed and more settled about the situation.

He explained to his wife that he thought about it and decided that he would lift the one match ban but he needed an audience between Ashton and his mother before he gave his final verdict on the situation. On the other hand, he was preparing to meet the person who sent the video of his daughter doing drugs and acting out of character.

The scene was set and he went inside not having a clue who the person was because of the different activities that's taking place. He got a call which the person instructed sit at table 5 and make an order don't hang up this is how we communicate. Show yourself or else I'm leaving the mystery man sends the video to him and said, "You leave and everyone in here gets the video." He sat back down and made an order. "Ok so what's the ransom," he chuckled, "I don't need your money I'm just here to expose to you the type of person your daughter is, oh and I am aware of all the cops inside and around the restaurant so you already breech the agreement. Don't worry I'll reward you for your insolence."

The headmaster acted surprised and that he didn't have a clue about what he was talking about and the phone hang up. Shortly after he got up before he received his order stunned because his daughter called him crying saying she got a text that the video would be released on Friday because her father isn't a man of his words.

He went on outside walked to his car and drove off without saying a word to anyone with his mind lost in wonderland. He ran into a stoplight and got hit by a truck. His friend, detective Palmer rushed to the scene where he saw his childhood friend laying in his car almost lifeless with blood everywhere. He radio in the accident, got help and took his friend to the hospital where he was in critical condition.

That same night his wife went out searching for the mystery man all by herself almost catching up to his real identity. She got mugged and fell in a coma and was later found that day by some kids running in the Alley [T1]. She got help and was rushed to the hospital in critical condition. Detective Jack Palmer knowing all this information immediately thought about Alecia and called her up not breaking the news to her as yet. He went onto ensuring if she was fine. He went and got her from the movies where she was with her two friends Kylie and Sofia. She was somewhat shock in the manner that her Uncle Palmer came to her in such a manner looking dazed. She asked if everything is fine and he didn't even reply. He went on driving taking her to his house where she went in and saw his wife Grace Palmer and her 2 daughters Kelsey and Ashley aged 10 and 13 respectively. She started to feel anxious about the situation and started asking questions. "Is everything OK?" "Am I in some sort of trouble?" Because I told my mom I was going to the movies with Kylie and

Sofia. Jack walked out angry seeing Alicia's innocence about to be taken from her once his wife breaks the news to her. "Ally baby you did nothing wrong," Grace said in a cracking voice.

"Then why did uncle Palmer came to me at the movies with my friends? You know, he didn't even speak to me on the journey. I knew I made a mistake but everyone's looking at me and treating me as if I killed someone. I'm only 18. People do make mistakes." "No baby it isn't about what you did," Grace looked at Jack and he nodded his head asking her the go ahead to break the news to Alicia.

"Here's the thing, you might wanna sit for this," Grace said. "You guys are really scaring me right now." "I don't know how to break this to you but your mom was found mugged in Alley last night and brought to the hospital and your dad got in an accident earlier in the night after meeting the guy blackmailing him about releasing the video of you at Trenton's party. Both are at the hospital right now in critical condition receiving treatment." After getting this news Alicia felt light headed and almost falling to the ground where she was held up by Grace and Jack where they brought her to the living room for resuscitation.

She cried for hours not eating and not speaking to anyone for 2 days. Ash got to hear about this from Conny because Jack reached out to him thinking he and Alicia were still a thing. Conny told Ash after the training session. Ash went to her house after the session where he saw detective Jack Palmer scouting out the premises. "Hey what are you doing here?" Jack said. "I'm here to see Alicia," Ash replied. Being a bit confused he asked, "Why isn't she Conny's girlfriend?" "They broke up couple weeks ago and we started to see each other after that." Being confused he told Ashton where he can find her. Ash went on to school and training where coach Murrey was going to list the players who were eligible for the game on Friday base off the USADA results. Coach Murrey, "OK as you know we undergo some purification test for the team and the players that are Eligible in the 18-man squad for this Friday are;

1. GK- Deandre Steele
3. CB- Joe Douglas
5. CB- George Ruddy
13. LB- Rolando Small
2. RB- Adrian Peterson
8. CM- Michael Brooks
6. CM- Maleek Walls
10. CAM- Ashton Allen (C) (Ash)
22. RM- Xavier Henry
11. LM- John Headley
18. CF- Martin Michelson
27. GK- Liam Brown
40. GK- Jacob Henderson
33. CB- Elijah Reed
20. CM- William Hill
14. DM- Noah Green
25. CAM- Oliver Drake
7. RM- Lucas Naldo
15. LM- Benjamin Grover
23. CAM- James Love

66. RB- Daniel Logan

16. LB- Christian Trump

These players are to remain:

Treyon James

Andre Johnson

Conroy Wilson

See you guys tomorrow for our last training session before Friday." "Coach why isn't Ashton here with us?" Dre uttered. "Oh yes Ashton you should remain also. You're all dismissed see you tomorrow. You guys failed the USADA test Can you explain to me how my 3 starting 11 players failed a drug test?" Coach Murrey said angrily. "I thought Ash failed also, that's why you told him to remain," Dre said. "Now why would you think that? He is here because he is the team Captain and I need answers." Dre was surprised that Ashton didn't fail the test also because he spiked his water bottle with creatine in the dressing room but what he didn't know is that Steven was in the dressing room waiting for Ashton to surprise him at half time where he heard someone coming and hiding.

He realized it was Dre and was going to show himself but what he saw him doing was best he remained hidden until he is through. After watching Dre spiked his own water bottle and some of his teammates. He waited until he knew the coast was clear and dispose of all the water bottles, he saw him spiking and replaced them with fresh water excluding his. Trenton and Conny only failed because they had a drink from Dre's water bottle. Steven didn't tell Ash because he never wanted to create a bad energy amongst the players after seeing them reach this far so he withheld the information from his brother until further notice.

Coach Murrey spoke to the players and he told them he can make an appeal for them to retake the test and still have a chance to compete in the Finals on Friday. He told the boys to drink lots of water to purge out their system and exercise to help them maintain their fitness and dismissed them. Ashton who thought it was a little suspicious how Dre was almost certain that he would fail the doping test started to wonder why he was so sure he was going to fail along with them.

Chapter 5
FACING THE FIRE

After training Ash went onto seeing Alicia at detective Palmer's house where she was staying for protection. He rang the doorbell and Grace came out to greet him. "Hello good afternoon I am here to see Alicia," "Good afternoon, Ash, she isn't taking any visitors right now," "Just do me a favor and tell her Ash is here to see her," "Ok, she turned down Sofia and Kylie's visit but I'll let her know you are out here. Give me a sec." Grace went upstairs and knocked on her room saying, "Hey pumpkin Ash is here to see you. I can send him home if you want me to." And for the first time in two days, she opened her room door and told her to send him up. Grace was shocked, she replied, "Ok", and went on down to send him up.

Alicia began to clean up as best as she can to accommodate Ash because her room was a mess. He went up and knocked on her door twice and she came out looking distress. "Hey how are you doing, beautiful?" She replied; "Not so well", and before she could finish what she had to say he gave her a warm hug and tears began streaming down her face while he comforted her.

This was what she wanted in her fragile state of mind. Someone to be there. No questions just their presence and a warm embrace. "You hungry? cause I'm starving. I brought your favourite," Ash said. "Tacos!!!" "Yes, I brought Tacos I know how much you love Mexican food so I got you some Tacos." She almost felt like herself again for the first time since the accident and her mother's mugging. He spent the night in her room because she fell asleep laying down in his arms where she felt safe.

Grace went up there a few times to ensure that they are OK where she saw Alicia laying there sleeping in Ashton's arms. Later that night Steven and Trey went to Jack's place where Trey saw Dre and Conny and he went over to greet them both while Steven hang back looking at Dre with a straight face. "I heard a lot about you guys, Dre and Conny right," "Who's asking?" Conny uttered. The guys continued to speak for a while before Trey walked away and met Steven. "Those guys are Ashton's best friend," "Best friends, I see," Steven then spoke in another language, "A really yuh fren dem can really hurt yuh." Trey being confused on why he said that asked him why he would say something like that and he told him about what he saw in the dressing room upon surprising Ash on the halftime break.

Treyon started to track back on that day that he really saw Dre under the tunnel and was wondering why is he down here and the game is in action. He got furious and wanted to confront Dre but Steven calmed him down and showed him the delicacy of the situation before he made his move. "I felt the same way but I can't confront him as yet or even speak to Ash about it because of the state championship, so it's better for us to keep it a secret until the season is through which is this Friday ok." "Ok" Trey replied with a sulking face. Both guys walked out and began heading home. Beep!!! Beep!!!! Beep!!! Ash jumped up and saw his phone alarming. He was confused at first about where he was not seeing. He got 13 missed calls from his mother and a couple from Steven and Trey. "I'm a dead man," he whispered to himself.

His mother called Detective Palmer and he and his wife already notified her about his location letting her know he is in safe hands. He began looking for his shoes without waking Alicia because she hasn't been getting any rest recently, so this was the first she slept in a while. So, he had to be as discreet as possible gathering his stuff to leave.

He finally found everything he was looking for and before leaving he wrote a note and kissed her on her forehead before heading out to meet his fate at home. "Sorry I had to leave in such short notice but I have to prepare myself for school. See you later. It was nice to meet, yah. If I'm dead when I get home and see my Mum P.S. Ashton," with a heart drawn at the bottom of the paper. While heading out he ran into detective Palmer and greeted him a good morning. He replied, "Good luck," Ash didn't even reply because he know he was a walking dead man on his way going home.

He walked out and began jogging on his way home. "Such a good kid," detective Palmer whispered to himself because he knew his mother was really upset with him. Ash finally got home and tried to sneak his way in at 5:33 am moving as stealthy as possible and out of nowhere he heard, "Ashton Jason Allen", he froze for about five seconds and turned around and saw his Mum looking at him. He was so frightened that immediately he started to explain what made him miss all those calls and slept out without running it by her. "Go get ready for school because we have somethings we need to talk about," "OK mum I love you." She replied, "Mhmm."

He got ready for school saw his breakfast was well prepared, had breakfast, kissed his mom on the cheeks and head out. Steven got up that morning and got a call from his girlfriend saying she will be coming to visit him on Friday and but she needs him to get her at the airport by 6pm. He never told anyone his girlfriend was coming to visit because he wanted it to be a surprise because his mom kept on asking him when will he introduce his girlfriend to the family. Later that day, Ash arrived at school feeling rejuvenated. He went to his classes and met up with coach Murrey and the squad in the dressing room. "Ok guys settle down we have some good news, I've made and appeal for Conny, Dre and Trenton at USADA and got the go ahead to let them participate in tomorrow's game." The guys began cheering and feeling elated. "However, they will be undergoing some test at the end of the season to ensure that we haven't been using performance enhancement drugs throughout the season, so as of from now we eat at home for the next 2 weeks.

No drinking or eating out side of your household so that means No restaurants, No grills and No fast foods. Do I make myself clear?" They replied; "Yes Coach!!" The boys went out on the pitch after the meeting with Coach Murrey. They had a 40 minutes training session where he focused mainly on finishing and penalties. After a productive session the guys gather and had a word of prayer before hitting the showers and head home. "Remember to stay hydrated and get enough rest for tomorrow because it will be a life changing game for you guys." Coach Murrey shouted.

Ash stayed back for a bit, while showing Coach Murrey some playing styles of their opponents. 12 times state champions Eastern Academy who has 8 players who represents the country at the national level. Coach Murrey smiled and told Ash that he commends his love for the game and embrace his role as captain. "I did my research and went over all these videos but you highlighted something that went over my head seeing this video, their style of play is very unorthodox where seeing how they transition from defense to offense. One of their center backs turns in to a central midfielder while attacking overloading the midfield while creating a balance, but if you look at their shape defensively a well-placed pass through the channels can hurt the team." Coach Murrey sat down and thinking over his game plan after watching the video Ash showed him thinking that Ashton is a genius. "OK take care, coach. I'll see you tomorrow," Ash said before leaving. He went on home where he saw his mom sitting down outside waiting for him so they can clarify what happened yesterday. "Hey Mom, good evening. Listen, I know what I did wasn't right and there is no explanation for it but all I have to say is that I won't let it happen again." She smiled and look at him and said; "I am not angry with you because I heard what happened to both her parents and what she's been going through. Detective Palmer and his wife came over and apologized on your behalf.

I told them, it is OK I raised you right and for me to know that you mean so much to someone else, I am very proud of you, my boy." He hugged his mom and went inside and had dinner with his siblings and cousin. Ash's mom wasn't feeling well and went to the doctor where she did some test and the results came back today and she found out she had stage 5 lung cancer and had 5 months maximum, if placed on extensive care.

She found out she had cancer 2 years ago and began treating it as best as possible while keeping it a secret from her kids because she didn't want them to be worried and lose focus in school. When she found out that it has been getting worse, she couldn't risk using up her children's college tuition for her health.

So she started to use home remedies to help her ease the pain. She has been feeling over the past few months. She endured a lot, raising all four kids on her and even managed to save One Hundred Thousand Dollars in inheritance for her kids after she passed. She sat outside while the kids where inside eating and having a good time together. She looked inside and tears started streaming down her face. She whispered, "I am very grateful for everything you have done for me God, to be able to see my babies growing up.

I am not ready to leave them but if it is in your will let it be done, help them not to segregate but form a bond so tight that even on bad days they'll come through for each other. I thank you for my life and the lessons taught in your name. I pray, Amen." Whipped her tears and went inside with a broad smile and joined in the fun with everyone.

Chapter 6
CHOICES

Ashton went to bed that night 10:15 pm and began praying at his bed side for an injury match and for everyone who's going to participate in tomorrow's game even his opponents and went to bed after. Alicia finally came out of her room while Grace and Jack were in the living room watching a movie together they heard the footsteps, looked back and saw her.

They were so surprised at seeing her out her room for such a long time that they stop watching the movie immediately and turned their attention to her. "Look who decided to join us," said Detective Palmer. "Stop! You might startle her and she might not speak to us again." "You guys know that I'm right here." She replied; "And I'm not a deer in hunting season where you have to be discreet in approaching me." "Wow hunny, she's speaking also.

Let's get closer and see how she reacts," Alicia started wondering if it was her or the Palmer's were getting off and said, "Again I'm right here. I can hear you." They walked up near to her and she started looking at them before Grace gave her a warm embrace and she appreciated it. She thanked Grace and Jack for being so understanding and patient with her. It was finally game day and Ashton woke up exactly at 4:35 am, did his morning routine and hit the shower at 5:40 am.

He began speaking to himself and repeatedly affirming that he is a champion. "I am a champion and I claim it in your name," he repeated this about ten (10) times before getting out of the shower and getting dress for school. His mother and Steven woke up early ensuring that everything was smooth sailing for him before he left for school.

On his way to school, he stopped by at Conny's and Dre's houses to see if they were up and leaving for school. He was walking to the door where he saw Conny, Dre and Trenton having a talk and overheard Dre saying; "Who is this guy thinking he can wear my armband in the final, the most important game of the season.

If we won he will be known as the one who captained our team and lead us to victory. I say we place a bet on the Finals and play according to our bets and get some cash off this game who is in?" Ash felt so betrayed that one of his best friends could ever think like that, willing to sacrifice his team for something as trivial as an armband.

He didn't even ring the doorbell, he walked away feeling depressed and overwhelmed so he started praying; "Heavenly father as I come before you today, I just want to thank you for revealing and removing people from my life that doesn't mean me any good.

Even though it is a hard pill to swallow, don't stop until there is enough room made for the ones who should be here. I give you all the glory in your mighty name. I pray, Amen." Ash walked to school that day feeling somewhat depressed and anxious at the same time because scouts from all over the world will be there eyeing some young talents for recruiting. So he knew he had to be on his A game today.

Coach Murrey and the squad met up at 11:30 am where they went over the game plan and was about to name the starting 11 for today's game. "OK guys settle down, settle down the starting 11 for today's game will be as followed: In goal we will have Deandre Steele, at left back Rolando Small, in the right back position Daniel Logan, our two centre halves for today will be Andre Johnson our vice-captain and Joe Douglas, playing defensive midfield will be Noah Green and Maleek Walls, our Captain and attacking midfielder for today is Ashton Allen, Lucas Naldo and John Headley will be providing support from the wings and then our talisman upfront will be Conroy Wilson.

So that's our starting 11 today, we've made some changes from our last match which we gave a lot of thought but this will be our final squad for today. So go have lunch the school bus leaves at 1pm for our game at 6pm." The guys cheer and began to move to the gym for lunch. Ashton walked up to Dre, Trenton and Conny and said," Are you guys ok? You've been a little distant lately and we are best friends.

Let's just put all this behind us and focus on winning the match today because for some of us this will be a life changing game so let's put all this behind us and help each other accomplish the task ahead," "Giving speeches, I see real captain fantastic," Dre uttered and laugh sarcastically, it's all good bro this game is more important to me than anything else," Ash smiled and walked away.

Coach Murrey saw them speaking and began smiling knowing that everyone plays apart in the team but these four are his standout players and will surely be missed next season because they complement each other's style of play so brilliantly. The guys then board the bus and began heading to the National Arena where the Finals has been playing for the past few years.

Upon arriving the 3rd place, the playoff was going to be in action in the next half hour. Coach Murrey and the boys head to their respective areas but while on the way, they sense the presence of the Arena which was filled with different Academics and people from all over the country gathered to either watch Alame Academy make history or Eastern Academy claim another victory and add another silver wear to their cabinet.

The guys felt the atmosphere and some began to catch cold feet because they never played in an arena like this before with such a huge crowd. It was the first for Ash but he kept it cool and went inside the dressing room where coach Murrey was going over the final instructions for the game plan.

The third-place playoff was almost over where North East Academy led 2 goals to 1 against last year's runner up South Academy both teams went at it hammer to tongue up until the final minute where North East Academy came out victorious. Ash led the Alame Academy boys on the pitch where they were going to warm up before the game both teams were on either side of the pitch.

The East Academy boys were looking much more confident team, going into the warm up with their captain Jake Rodriguez who has been representing the senior team at the age 16 currently eighteen (18) being the only teen breaking ground into the men's senior team who also has seventeen (17) caps with five (5) assist and eight (8) goals is also an attacking midfielder who style of play resembles Kevin De Bruyne (KDB) of Manchester City. Most of the Alame Academy players admire him greatly and was somewhat of a fan because he's currently living the dream most of these boys wished they could live. It is even said he was linked with German giants Borrusia Dortmund.

Ash kept on motivating his teammates boosting their confidence during the warm up session before heading back to the dressing room. Ash kept on looking for his mom and siblings before heading down the tunnel he looked in the crowd but they were waiting on him at the dressing room.

Later he went down in the tunnel where he saw everyone waiting to see him one last time before he goes out on the pitch. He asked his mom where is Steven and she told him he was here a minute ago but he'll surely be there in time. He shook his head and went inside the dressing room. "Well, it's almost time my boys. I just want you guys to know regardless of the results I am very proud of you and you're all champions in my eyes so let's go out there and do what we've been doing from the starting of the season!!!" The boys cheered on and began to believe in themselves more, despite the inexperience.

Ash gathered the team and coaching staff and everyone took part by saying the lord's prayer. Then began marching out through the tunnel where the other team was already there, ready to go. Alecia wasn't mentally prepared to face the real world as yet, so she stayed home and set out to watch the game on her television.

She was one of Ashton's loyal supporters who never missed a game he played and cheered him wholeheartedly. This was the first game she wasn't there in person but she knew that Ash would understand her reasons not to be there. Both teams walked out the tunnel and a loud ROAR!!! came from the crowd.

Some of the boys became nervous while others couldn't wait until the game began. It was announced that everyone should stand for the US National Anthem and everyone stood up in the stadium and began singing.

Ash won the toss and chose to keep position of the ball. The atmosphere in the stadium was tense but yet vibrant and full of life. Alame Academy boys had a point to prove that they weren't a team to be slept on while the Eastern Academy boys had to show, why they are the favorites in this competition.

Ash gathered with the boys one last time for a team talk before the match went on its way. "Listen up, team! Today is our day. We've worked tirelessly to get to this moment, and I know we have what it takes to succeed. Remember why we started playing this beautiful game? For the love of it! For the thrill of competition, the rush of adrenaline, and the sense of accomplishment.

We are a team, a family. We support each other, we lift each other up, and we fight for every ball. We don't give up. We don't lose faith. Our opponents may be tough, but we are tougher. We've faced adversity before, and we've come out on top.

We've got the skills, the talent, and the determination. So, here's the plan: we go out there, we give it everything we've got, and we leave it all on the field. No regrets, no excuses. We play for each other, for ourselves, and for the pride of our team. Are you with me?!"

"Hell Yea!!!"

The guys shouted feeling a greater sense of belief and purpose. Ash whispered to himself, "God, I know you are always with me but I need you today more than ever. Guide my every move on this pitch and let each and every one of us come out this game victorious in our own way and injury free. Amen."

The game went on its way where the Alame Academy boys held position of the ball for a minute before playing a long pass towards Conny who held unto it beautifully awaiting support from his Captain and wing players he laid it off to Ashton who then moves past one, skipped past another one and played a brilliant ball out wide for Lucas Naldo who tried to whipped it across the face of the goal but his effort was blocked by Toby Weather who concedes the first corner of the game.

Ash went across to take it an out swing delivery inside the box trying to pick out one of his center halves. Ashton stepped up and sat the ball down before holding his right hand up doing a hand signal which stated to the Alame Academy boys that he will go deep with this corner kick.

The whistle blew and Ash whipped the ball over towards the back post where Dre and Dougy (Joe Douglas) were lurking to latch on to the delivery. "Ashton with a wicked delivery towards the back post, and it's Joe Douglas!!!!, Calvin Grey from off the line!!!" Dougy latch onto the cross winning the header putting it on target only to have it cleared by Calvin Grey off the line.

The stadium erupted with mixed emotions some fans thought it had crossed the line before the clearance was made while other's argued that it never went in. Coach Murrey thought it had went in also because he was furious at the 4th official who told him to calm down before he alerted the referee of his gestures towards him.

It was pretty much a free-flowing game up until the 28th minute where Noah Green played a brilliant ball over the top which Conny latched onto going 1v1 with the goalkeeper. He held off the defender brilliantly but couldn't convert the opportunity from 14 yards out.

He went for placement and the ball hit the bar and went over with the game locked at nil-nil (0-0). The Alame Academy boys started out on top in this game with more ball possession and chances created but the only thing missing from their game was the finishing product otherwise from that they were looking sharp and very well compacted as a team, defending in numbers and keeping their shape really well, when off the ball not giving the opponents a look in.

It was not until the 43rd minute the Eastern Academy boys got a free kick, 32 yards out with their dead ball expert Tyrell Simpson stepped up. He had scored 8 of his 10 free kicks throughout the season in hopes of making it 9 from 11, dead ball situations.

He spotted the ball then the referee blew the whistle. He waited for 4 seconds before whipping the ball up and over the wall forcing a save from goalkeeper Deandre Steele who touched the ball onto the post hitting the upright going out for a goal kick after Jordan Evans pounced on the rebound putting it wide off the target. The game went on for four (4) more minutes before the referee blew for halftime.

Chapter 7
THE LAST LAP

Alecia who was watching the game on the television got a call from the hospital that her father has finally woken up. She quickly got dress and told her aunt Grace who was also at home with her. They drove to the hospital. Alecia was really happy that her dad woke up and couldn't wait to get to the hospital.

They finally arrived and Alecia ran out of the car as soon as Grace got a parking spot. Grace wasn't even surprised because she knew how much she loves her dad. She ran into the waiting area went to the receptionist asking where can she find Alvin Reid and they told her before the receptionist could give her the directions, she ran off with no clue on finding where her dad was. She finally stopped running and asked a nurse where she can find room B14 and they directed her and send her on her way again. When she got inside the room, she gently pushed the door where she saw her father sitting upright. Before she could even catch her breath, her father said; "Come here baby girl, and give your Pops a hug," she couldn't hold it back anymore. Tears started rushing down her face feeling the warm embrace of her dad in over two (2) weeks. She just stood there hugging her dad, crying as if she was a toddler all over again.

He kissed her on the forehead and kept on repeating, "Don't cry my Munchkin, Daddy is here. Don't cry my Munchkin, Daddy is here." Even though he was in pain, he held his daughter to give her the comfort she needed. Steven on the other hand missed the first half of the game because he went to the airport to get his girlfriend, soon to be fiance Sophia.

When he came to the stadium, he went right beside his younger siblings, Trey and his mom awaiting the second half of this enticing game like everyone else. The atmosphere around the stadium was amazing, something Ash and his teammates never felt before.

The guys leave the pitch and went to the dressing room where Coach Murrey was upset at the chances that weren't converted and spoke about it. He also spoke to Ash who was rather silent in this game saying he was getting outshine by Jake Rodriguez in the midfield and told to step up his game.

The boys took what coach Murrey had to say and mentally implementing it in their game because it is said that in football, it is ninety percent (90%) mental and ten percent (10%) physical. It was almost time for the second half of the game where the Eastern Academy boys were lined up in the tunnel, awaiting their coach and captain in the dressing room.

The squad then went and find their way on the pitch doing some pre-second half warm ups, while the Alame Academy boys were doing some short sprints to warm up for the second half getting the guys back in their groove. They had to defend and keep their shape this time around because Eastern Academy would be the team to kick start the second half. The Alame Academy boys didn't know what Eastern Academy had plan at the start of the second half that would require them to sit back and not press the ball as expected.

As the whistle blew, Shane White to Nigel Ellis who then pass it to Jake Rodriguez who played a brilliant ball over the top for Spencer Sinclair who dispatches it beautifully. The score is now Eastern Academy one (1) Alame Academy zero (0). The stadium erupted with cheer to see such a brilliant play from the youngsters of the east. It was breath taking to say the least. Coach Murrey remained calm and sent instructions to his Captain and he grasped them and had a look in his eyes. He gathered his players and said, "OK guys, they took the lead now we have to out run, out pass, out score and out play them.

We won many games trailing behind earlier in the season. Let's show them that we are not here to lose LET'S GO!!!" The Alame Academy boys got fired up and got back into formation awaiting the restart of the game. The whistle blew and Ashton went on a rampage out playing everyone on the female as if he was a 15-years old at his peak playing against U9 players.

He completely took the game in hand setting up the equalizer, assisting Conny who latched onto a through pass which completely ripped the Eastern Academy boys back line in half allowing Conny to face the goalkeeper 1v1 who didn't hesitate to punish them this time around. "Now with the game settled at 1 apiece, let's see who wants it the most." The commentators expressed.

Both coaches were on the side-line shouting instructions and the match was very intense and interesting. Ashton on the ball moves pass one, moves pass two and played it to Headley, back to Ashton who plays it back to Headley, Conroy to Ashton who plays it out wide to Lucas Naldo 1v1 with Spencer Jones. Naldo go the best of him and used his left back overlapping run as a decoy to get more space for a brilliant pass inside the box aiming for the penalty spot where Ashton was lurking.

Ashton with a brilliant first touch got pass 1, moves pass 2 one versus one (1v1) with the goalkeeper. He moves the ball around him even though the goalkeeper came and made himself big Ashton got pass him staring an empty net. He held his nerve and slotted the ball inside an empty net leaving everyone astonished. "Oh, what a mesmerizing sight! He's got the ball on a string! The way he's gliding past defenders, leaving them in his wake... it's like a hot knife through butter. This is a masterclass in dribbling, folks! He's making it look effortless, but we know the hours and hours of practice that have gone into honing this skill.

Truly, a delight to behold!" The commentator expressed. Even some of the opposition fans were clapping the skill that Ashton displayed to score the goal. He stunned everyone. Coach Murrey knew he had it in him but even he was surprised by the composure shown by Ashton for the team's go-ahead goal.

He got on his knees and pointed to the sky in celebration of his goal. Ashton looked to the stands where he knew his mom and siblings were and blew a kiss to them. The game had restarted with Alame Academy regaining position and playing keep ball slowly breaking down the Eastern Academy boys shape defensively.

They made a total of thirty-eight (38) consecutive passes before playing a pass through the lines for Conny to latch on, which he did to force a save from the goal keeper. The match got very enticing both teams started to go after it, so it became an end to end battle for the championship until the seventy third minute where Ashton went on a solo run leaving five defenders in his wake before playing a beautiful pass out wide towards Lucas Naldo who latch onto it who played it back on top for Ashton who went to pull the trigger but got caught from behind by one of the opponents who received a straight red card for the challenge that he made on Ashton. "ARGH!!!!!" Ash groan in pain while holding his Ankle he rolled about three (3) times.

Before stopping and holding his ankles, he was in so much pain that everyone thought he had broken his ankles, his white socks became soaked in red from his blood that was pouring out his ankles from the tackle made from behind by the Eastern Academy defender.

They were signaling the medics but he told them no. He'll seek medical attention and a change of sock after the free kick right on top of the 18 yards box. The scouts who were there admired his resilience and determination to carry on after such a robust tackle. He clench his fist and force his self-up with the bleeding being stopped temporarily the referee told him that he needs to exit the pitch until he changes his socks but he told him he would leave voluntarily after this free kick.

Ash went and spotted the ball and took three (3) steps back and took a deep breathe "Phwwwwwhht." The whistle blew, he held his breathe for four (4) seconds before stepping up to the ball and whipping it into the top right hand corner of the goal leaving the goalkeeper with no chance. And Ashton steps up with a peach of a left foot and he stepped up and put it up and over, "WHAT A GOAL!!!! MARVELOUS HE PICKED HIS SPOT AND BANGED IT INTO THE TOP RIGHT HAND CORNER 2-1." The commentator shouted the cheering of the crowd echoed across the entire stadium for Ashton and the Alame Academy boys.

Even some scouts celebrated the free kick as if it was one of their own had scores.

"From 1 goal down to an impressive 2-1 lead, the Alame Academy boys have the game in hand," the commentators expressed. Some of the opposition team members started asking why wasn't Ashton removed from the field despite needing treatment and a new pair of socks.

Even the coaching staff got involved leaving the referee with no choice but to book a couple staff members and two (2) players on the bench for their behavior towards him and his officials. The game went on free flowing until the eighty eighth(88th) minute Eastern Academy got a penalty through a handball inside the six (6) yard box from a corner kick.

The Alame Academy boys all put their faith and support inside their shot stopper Deandre Steele who is facing one of the best, if not the best penalty taker in the league Jake Rodriguez, looking as poised as ever, facing the best shot stopper in the league this year Deandre Steele. The referee went on and blew the whistle and JR (Jake Rodriguez) took a deep breathe waited for four (4) seconds and with short run up to the ball. Having the ball saved by Deandre Steele, the crowd went wild and Deandre's teammates ran onto him and celebrated wildly before the referee got a signal from the linesman that Deandre was off his line before the ball was touched by JR. He was booked and the penalty was taken over. "And JR looking rather nervous on his second time around focusing on beating Deandre Steele," "Phwwwwwhht," the whistle blew he took another deep breath and waited for four (4) seconds again before stepping up. "And it's Jake Rodriguez for the second time around, SAVE!!! by Deandre Steele and the rebound pounced on by JR who celebrated wildly after locking the game at 2-2."

The crowd got excited never have they seen such an end to end game up until the final minute. The fourth official signaled five (5) minutes added time. On the other hand, Alecia was speaking to her dad and he asked why isn't his wife here with her, if she is upset with him for being in the hospital.

She broke down in tears leaving her Dad confused on why she was crying and he asked, "What's the matter Munchkin, why are you crying?" She answered, "The day you had the accident mom went out searching for clues about who had been blackmailing her and they saw that she was onto them and mugged her.

She is currently in extensive care." Her dad looked in surprise and almost had a heart attack hearing the news. He tried getting up but failed because of the damage he with-stand in the accident. He begged the doctors to let him see his wife and screamed out her name while they tried calming him down.

Alecia watched her father crying and consoled him. The game got pretty intense where both teams are going after it, up until the ninety third minute, when the ball got cleared from a brilliant counter attack and Lucas Naldo who was furthest up the pitch latched onto the ball and kept it waiting on his teammates to break between the lines.

He played a perfectly waited ball through to Ashton who is onside now facing the keeper in a 1v1 battle. Everyone got on their feet, Ashton against the goalkeeper who will win that battle. "Ashton dribbles, he steps up and..."

www.ingramcontent.com/pod-product-compliance
Lightning Source LLC
LaVergne TN
LVHW061602070526
838199LV00077B/7140